THE ADVENTURES OF
NINJA KID

By Deb and Cole Patterson

Illustrated by Katie Heady

THE ADVENTURES OF
NINJA KID

Copyright © 2016 by Deb and Cole Patterson
Artwork by: Katie Heady

ISBN: ISBN-13: 978-1523960767
ISBN-10: 1523960760

Contact: Find us on Facebook at
The Adventures of Ninja Kid

Printed in U.S.A

This book is lovingly dedicated to
The Rat Stalker.

CHAPTER 1

Hey there! My name is Chris, and I just turned 11 two days ago. I'm a pretty normal kid. I have a dog, a too-early bedtime, and I live in a boring, beautiful town in Southern California. I lead a fairly uninteresting life. But, it wasn't always that way. Oh no. It was once very different. VERY diffcrent. I'll tell you all about that. But first, there are three important things you really should know about me.

1. I love snickerdoodle cookies. Well, really, who doesn't? They are basically cinnamon perfection.

2. My mom is TOTALLY overprotective. She won't even let me ride my bike with my best friend to the park. She says she has to drive us. She says she worries. Ugh! Which brings me to...

3. I'm a ninja.

Okay, that last one might need a little explaining. How is an 11 year old kid in suburbia a ninja? With an overprotective mom? Well, it's kind of a wild story, so buckle your seat belt! Here goes…

✦✦✦

When I was little, my mom, dad, and I lived in Japan. We lived out in the country, in a green, shining land next to a ninja training compound. The air always felt slightly cool, and a mist that would cover the ground and curl around bushes like a snake would hang around all evening into the morning. My dad was a hot shot scientist, working in this cutting edge lab.

One night, Mom took me to visit Dad in the lab. I was just a little kid, a baby really. Dad wanted to show us this top secret gene he was developing in rats, one that would make it possible for them to work their way down in the rubble of buildings that had collapsed in earthquakes, helping to find survivors. It was really fantastic work. He was going to change the world!

I recall being in the lab, and Dad showing us the project and talking excitedly. It was so close to completion! I remember Mom and Dad talking in hushed voices, and my dad handing something small to my mom, and her putting it in her pocket. Then she and Dad left me in a playpen in the corner. There was something else in the other room Mom wanted to see. Dad kissed me. "I love you, Kiddo! Mom and I will be right back!"

Those were the last words my dad ever said to me.

As Mom and Dad walked out of the room, out of the shadows, a gangly man in a puke yellow exterminator suit appeared, took his shovel, and hit my mom in the back of the head. She thudded heavily to the floor, silent. As my dad turned to help, the exterminator then shoved the sharp edge of the tool against my dad's throat.

"You!" he said! "YOU are the one trying to destroy my business! If you make rats good and lovable, no one will ever want to get rid of them! I am the RAT STALKER,

pest exterminator extraordinaire! This is my LIFE! Rats must be evil, so I can destroy them! You must die!"

As I watched in horror, the Rat Stalker pushed my dad out of the room. I heard a loud bang, saw a flash, and then an acrid burning smell filled my nose, like when my mom burned popcorn in the microwave. Smoke filled the room. My eyes watered, and I started to cough. Mom woke up and rushed me out of there, just in time.

Dad didn't make it.

Dad's death was ruled an accident. The reports read that a chemical mixture had exploded, and Mom thought that was why she passed out. She never realized she had been hit in the head. All that important work burned up in the lab that night. No one but me ever knew the truth, and I wasn't talking. In fact, I had other plans.

From then on, every day after that, while Mom thought I was napping, I sneaked out of my room on my tiny little legs and went next door to the ninja compound. I watched. I learned. Eventually, the ninjas accepted me as one of their own and let me train with them. I trained diligently. I was determined to become strong and capable. I was going to take that Rat Stalker DOWN!

Many years of practice later, after many supposed nap times, I was just about ready to take him on. I wasn't quite all the way trained, but I was strong, I was stealthy, and I was prepared! I just needed to work on my balance more to be fully accomplished. Okay, and maybe my stealth…and aim…and…but that's beside the point. The point is…then I got the news…we were moving back to America, without ever facing the Rat Stalker, without ever avenging my dad! I was so depressed. I gave up on ever getting justice.

★★★

So here we are. That's the story of number 3, and why I'm a ninja. Mom doesn't know. She thinks I'm just a normal kid in dirty sneakers, about to start the first day of 6th grade. We are basically happy together, mom and me and our dog. But I know she gets sad a lot. She cries when she thinks I can't hear her. She still misses my dad sometimes. Sometimes, so do I.

CHAPTER 2

"Chris! Breakfast!" Mom yelled. I ran down the stairs. At the bottom, I tripped over my laundry basket, and pin wheeled into the kitchen, arms and legs flying. My dog, Bok Choy, yelped as I accidentally stepped on her tail. She's kind of big, and hard to miss. "You didn't put your laundry away again, right?" Mom laughed, shaking her head.

"No. I'm sorry! I keep forgetting!" I said. As I sat down to eat my egg bagel and drink my orange juice (always with no pulp), Mom turned back to the counter to pour herself some more coffee in her favorite blue mug. The coffee splashed her hand. "Ouch! Dang it!" I watched as her coffee cup dropped and smashed into sharp pieces all over the tile floor. "I don't have time for this," she muttered. Mom bent down and started to clean up the mess.

While Mom was down on her hands and knees wiping up the spill, I heard the sound of our creaky side door opening. I looked at Bok Choy. She was totally oblivious, and licking her paw like it was a popsicle. She's not the best guard dog in the world.

Something caught my attention, and I looked up, my eyes widening in surprise. There, at the entrance to the kitchen, dressed all in black and carrying a large, sharp sword, a ninja stood threatening me with his eyes! One quick glance at Mom, still down on the floor with paper towels, and I knew I had to act.

Without thinking, I quickly bit my bagel into a sharp sided ninja star and flung it at the ninja with all my might. As it hit him in the eye, I jumped up, accidentally hitting the light fixture above our kitchen island, sending it swaying. I leaped towards him, grabbing a chair, and swinging it skillfully at his head. Bok Choy jumped out of the way. It hit the ninja with a thud, sounding like that time last week I threw a watermelon down the street for fun with my buddy Rover. The intruder fell backwards through the sliding glass door, causing sharp glass shards to land all over the floor.

As I watched, he got up, limping in terror, knocking over our flower pots on the patio, sending them clanking and spilling loamy dirt all over the bricks as he ran off.

Mom finally finished cleaning the mess, stood up, and turned around. "CHRISTOPHER!" she shrieked. Bok Choy backed slowly away, her tail wagging nervously.

"Yes, Mom?" I answered, smiling proudly, expecting to be praised. I should have known better when I heard

Mom use my full name.

"What the heck did you do?! The kitchen looks like it was hit by a tornado!"

"I just saved us from a ninja!" I stood tall and puffed my chest out a little. "Aren't you proud of me?" Mom narrowed her eyes and looked at me doubtfully.

"A ninja? Do you think I'm stupid? Why did you do this to the kitchen?"

"But Mom! He was just here! Didn't you see him?"

"All I see is a big mess. On top of my broken coffee cup, now this? We don't have time for this! Now clean it up quickly before you have to leave for your first day!" she said crossly. "I'll have to have that glass replaced." I heard her mutter under her breath. "And don't call me Butt Mom!" she yelled as she left the room to call the glass company.

After I cleaned up the mess, I had to rush to brush my teeth and put on my shoes. My shoes were easy, because I never untie the laces. I just slip them on. This means they're pretty loose all the time, and sometimes my shoe goes flying when I kick a ball at soccer during recess, but all in all, it's worth it not to have to tie them. I started to ponder who the heck had sent a ninja as I put them on, but then my mom yelled it was time to go. Thinking would have to wait.

We got in our car, and headed to school. At the entrance, Mom pulled over and parked. "Just drop me off! I'm not a baby!" I whined.

"I want to watch you walk in. I worry about you."

"Mom! I'm a ninja! I'm ok! Don't worry about me!" Mom shook her head.

"Enough with the ninja talk. That's ridiculous. I actually wanted to stop here for another reason, too." Mom looked kind of weird. Her eyes filled up with tears, and her voice got all quivery. "This is your first day of middle school. You're getting older. I wanted to give you something." Mom reached across past the coffee mug she had replaced from this morning, into the glove box.

14

She pulled out something small, metallic, and rusty. "This was your dad's, and his dad's before him."

"Is it a ninja star?" I wriggled in my seat like an excited puppy.

"No... I'm trying to be serious here!" Her eyes flashed a bit of irritation among the tears, something I was used to when I talked ninja. "It's Grandpa's lighter. He used to carry it around everywhere, and then so did your dad. I don't even think it works anymore. Your dad gave it to me the night he... the night of the fire. He would've wanted you to have it. You're old enough now." I took the lighter. It felt strangely heavy in my palm. It seemed almost to glow.

"Thanks...I guess. Kind of a weird present for an 11 year old, but ok." She smiled, and wiped away the tear that had dripped.

"Have a good first day. I'll pick you up later. I love you!" I got out, slammed the door, and waved. I then squared my shoulders, tucked the lighter in my back pocket for a good luck charm, and turned to face my first day of ~~prison~~ middle school.

CHAPTER 3

My first class was Home Economics. Mom made me sign up for it because she said I needed to know how live on my own when she kicked me out at eighteen. She was joking, I think. I'm not entirely sure.

Home Ec. is a class where they teach you stuff like cooking and cleaning and sewing... you know, sissy stuff. It sounded horrible. I was dreading it as I walked toward the classroom. My steps slowed, my feet shuffled, my head was down as I reached for the handle to open the door. It felt like it weighed two tons as I swung it open.

"Welcome, Dude! Aloha!" I heard as I stepped inside. I looked up, my eyes widening. In front of the class stood a young teacher, a young MALE teacher, wearing a Hawaiian shirt and a huge smile. "Take a seat! Anywhere! We're about to get started." As I sat down, I looked around in shock. The class wasn't all girls, as I expected. It was about half and half girls and boys, and everyone was smiling and talking to each other. Maybe this wasn't

going to be so bad after all!

"I'm Mr. Bulwark. I'm here to teach you how to survive on your own in the real world. Also, how to make an awesome lasagna! We're going to have fun!" As the class went on, we went around the room and everyone introduced themselves, and told about their cooking experiences. I didn't have much to tell, except for my famous peanut butter and jelly waffle sandwiches. They really are stellar. The warm waffles get the peanut butter a little melty, and the cold jelly balances it all out. The first bite feels like being in the front row of a roller coaster... but

I digress. Home Ec. turned out to be not so bad. And Mr. Bulwark was pretty cool. I left the classroom feeling a little better about school.

The rest of the morning continued uneventfully, with three more classes. English and PE were ok, but math was dreadfully, awfully horrible. At lunchtime, I went to my new locker, and tried to figure out how to work it. As I was turning the lock for somewhere around the eighth time- who's counting?- my best friend Rover danced up to me.

"Howdy y'all!" I raised an eyebrow and gave him a look. He's always saying weird things like that. "How's school going?"

"Ok, but I'm starving. And I can't figure out this lock. Let's go eat! I have to tell you what happened BEFORE school!" I gave up on my locker and carried my stuff with me as we walked to the cafeteria.

Rover is my best friend. His real name is Rodger. We met when I moved here from Japan. He lives on my street, and was lying on the sidewalk in front of my house, playing with a worm, the day we moved in. As I got out of the car, a cat passed by him. In a flash, he was up, chasing that cat down the street and up a tree. He reminded me of a big, sloppy sheepdog, with his loping gait and his hair in his eyes. When he came back to my house to say hi, my name is Rodger... all I heard was Rover. I've called him that ever since. Now, everyone else calls him Rover, too.

"Rover! You're never going to believe what happened this morning at breakfast!" As I told him the ninja tale, we gobbled our lunch as fast as we could. We didn't want to hang out in the cafeteria too long. It smelled like feet and sloppy joes, in that order.

"No way!" Rover said, after he heard the story. "A ninja! Who do you suppose sent him? Did you kick his butt?" Rover basically skipped in excitement out the door as he asked me the questions.

"I have no idea who could have sent him! Nobody but you even knows I'm a ninja! Well, my mom does, but she doesn't believe me when I tell her. So, no... just you! Who do you think it could be?"

"Hum... maybe someone from when you lived in Japan? That's the only thing that makes sense."

"Could be. What about..." Just then the bell rang. "Already? Lunch is so short in middle school! Okay, we'll talk about this more later. What class do you have next?" I asked. Rover pulled out his schedule.

"I have math." He did a strange air quote as he said math. He's so odd.

"History here. " I grimaced. "See you after school? We'll ride our bikes to the park. Ha ha, right." I said sarcastically. "Like Mom would ever let us. But we can figure out this ninja mystery then. Banzai!" We fist bumped.

"Banzai, dude!" Rover twirled and danced off to math.

I sighed. He was such a weird friend sometimes. Good, solid, dependable. But weird.

CHAPTER 4

The next morning I was almost late to school. I couldn't find any clean clothes. Mom had to remind me they were all still in my laundry basket, sitting at the bottom of the stairs. By the time I got dressed and got to my first class, Mr. Bulwark was just shutting the classroom door.

"Ohayou gozaimasu! Good morning! Glad you could make it!" Mr. Bulwark was dressed up like a Japanese sushi chef, with a white hat and everything.

"So we're going to cook today instead of learning?" I asked, with a smirk on my face.

"Cooking IS learning!" Mr. Bulwark answered, bowing deeply. "We will learn to make sushi, and learn a little bit about Japanese culture today. Fighting culture, perhaps?" He gave me a knowing smile. "And, maybe even learn a bit about manners, Smarty Pants." All I was thinking was, *What's that smile about?*

We started making sushi, and let's just say, it wasn't as pleasant as I thought it would be. They make it look so good in pictures, but the raw fish felt like frog skin, and it tasted... Ugh! How to explain it? Um... let's see... it tasted like the feeling you get when you hear the hiss of a creeper behind you in MineCraft. Not good, for those of you who don't play MineCraft. Not good at all! I may be a ninja, but I prefer pizza!

At lunchtime, I met up with Rover again.

"Greetings, earthling," he said in a robotic voice, holding up his hand like a Star Trek Vulcan.

"Hi Rover!" I said, sighing impatiently. "That's all you have to say." I told him. "One word. Hi. Not those crazy greetings!" He was so frustrating. "Let's go get some lunch." We into the cafeteria, and it smelled even worse than it did the day before. "Ugh! What IS that??"

"It's Tuesday Surprise," said the lunch lady in a raspy voice, slopping a spoonful of something that looked suspiciously like the color and texture of dog poop onto my plate. I swear I saw the plate starting to smoke. I quickly walked as fast as I could without getting yelled at by the lunch duty lady to the trash can, and dumped the food in. Then I poured my carton of "milk" on top, just to make sure it didn't catch fire. True ninja skills! No lunch for me today.

After school, Rover came home with me.

"Mom! We need something to eat! I'm famished!"

"Why so hungry? And is grilled cheese okay? I'd make you snickerdoodles, but I'm out of cinnamon."

We nodded as Mom pulled out cheese, bread, and margarine to make sandwiches.

"I didn't eat anything all day."

"Why not?" Mom furrowed her brow.

"Because the sushi was not pizza, and the Tuesday Surprise melted the tray."

"Oh right, and your homework was calculus and your teacher was Abraham Lincoln," Mom fired back. She never believes anything I say.

As we watched Mom make food, Rover opened his backpack and pulled out a mason jar filled with some grayish, hairy looking stuff. We ate looking at it. Rover collects belly button lint. None of it is his, or so he says. He gathers it from other people. He says it's for charity. What charity would like that, I don't know, but he keeps collecting it!

As Mom sat there eating with us, Rover said to her, "Do you have any spare belly button lint I could borrow, please?" She looked at him with narrowed eyes for a second, and then gave me a long stare.

Still looking at me, she replied in a flat tone, "No, Rover. I don't have any spare belly button lint. Now eat your food. I think I'll finish mine in the living room." She picked up her plate and walked away without a further word.

"Dude!" I raised my hands. "Stop asking for belly button lint! It's crazy! My mom thinks you're nuts!"

"Sorry! It's an addiction," he fired back, popping the last of the grilled cheese in his mouth. "Let's go to the park!" Rover suggested. "We can try to figure out who that ninja was there."

"Okay, but my mom won't let me ride my bike, remember?"

"Gosh, that is SO lame!"

"Oh, and belly button lint isn't?" I fired back. We grabbed some chips and headed for the door. Rover stopped, leaned down, and started to touch Bok Choy.

"Rover! NO! Don't try to get her belly button lint!" Rover put his hands high in the air.

"Hey, I was just petting her," he said, looking guilty. He backed away.

Mom drove us to the park. "Thanks, Mom! See you in a couple hours!" The breeze was strangely warm and silent in the park, and I could smell the eucalyptus in the air. As she drove away, I noticed something moving stealthily in the trees out the corner of my eye. *What was that?*

CHAPTER 5

I looked over to the trees, but didn't see anything. I glanced at Rover, and he had his shirt up, examining his belly button. "Rover! Did you see that?"

"Where? What? More belly button lint?"

"No! What was that movement in the tree?" As we watched, suddenly, a rat jumped off a low branch of the eucalyptus tree. It was followed by another. Then another! Then a whole swarm, pack, herd, whatever it is for rats! came rushing down out of the tree and headed straight for us! As the first one reached us, I reached out quickly with my ninja skills and scooped it up.

"Rover, fetch!" I threw the rat as far away as I could. Without hesitation, Rover ran off after the rat. *Good! I thought. He's safely out of the way.*

I turned back to face the large mass of rats heading for me, their beady eyes full of hatred. Two rats reached me at the same time. I felt their scaly paws as they started to rapidly climb up my pants leg. I grasped one in each hand, their furry bellies jiggling under my fingers.

I shivered. *Gross! I didn't sign up for this!* I grimaced. I grabbed their wormlike tails and tied the two together. I gave them a test swing. Now I was set. I had just invented Ratchucks! Just like nun-chucks, but a tad more awesome.

I turned to face the mob of angry rats with my Ratchucks in hand. "Banzai!" I cried, and began swinging away. WHAM! I hit about 10 rats in one sweep, sending them flying and squealing across the grass and into the road. THUD! The Ratchucks swept up a few more, and these went sailing over the fence into the backyard of the old couple who were always yelling at us to get off their lawn. "Oops!" I said, amused. I wasn't too sorry about that one.

I looked over at Rover. Currently, he was chasing the rat down the slide on the other side of the park. Little kids were watching him and jumping up and down and cheering. They weren't looking at me at all. They were completely focused on Rover.

I turned back to see the remainder of the rats, not many left, closing in on me in a circle. Banzai! I did one ninja sweep kick, and sent the rest of them flying back into the tree. I untied the Ratchucks, and gently set the two now unconscious rats down at the base of tree. "Sorry it had to end like this, friends. I kind of beat the crud out you. My father really respected you guys." As I said this last part, the lighter I carried with me from my

dad seemed to glow and feel hot in my pocket. It was strange and soothing all at once.

As I walked over to distract Rover and to let the poor last rat go, I saw a quick shadow jump out of the tree. It was large, like a man, but scampered like a rodent. It disappeared quickly into the grove of trees. I tried to watch it go, but Rover jumped on me.

"I almost had him!" He hooked an arm around my neck, laughing. He hadn't seen the fight at all!

"Rover! We were ambushed! WHO is doing this?"

"What are you talking about?!" As I explained the rat fight, we tried to figure out what was going on. We had no idea. We left the park later, when the sun went down, as much in the dark as the empty merry go round now sat.

CHAPTER 6

The next morning at school, the madness started again when Mr. Bulwark greeted us at the door with "Bonjour!" He was dressed in a white chef's outfit, like some crazy cartoon character. He had even drawn on a thin mustache over his upper lip with what looked like black marker.

"Let me guess," I said sarcastically, as I walked to my seat. "Cajun today?"

"Ooh la la!" he laughed giddily. "Close! Non! We are French today! But you knew that, you crazy ninja!" I startled, and turned back to look at him. My face dropped.

"What? What did you call me?" I asked.

"You crazy nin... nin... compoop! You crazy nincompoop! Go take your seat." Mr. Bulwark looked flustered, his voice suddenly serious, and his face flushed red.

How does he know I'm a ninja? Was he at the park? Is he the guy that attacked me in the kitchen? All these thoughts filled my head as I took my seat. But they were quickly drowned out by the sizzle of crepes cooking in many different pans across the room.

"Chris, I need to see you after class," Mr. Bulwark said, as he passed my station, startling me out of my thoughts. "And by the way, your crepe is burning." I gasped and turned back to my pan, and saw a cloud of black smoke rising up. I panicked, and frantically turned the knob to what I thought was off. Guess what? I'm an idiot! I turned it UP! The smoke billowed, and the flames grew higher, and spread to the crepe pan to my right. It started to smoke immediately, too. I saw it rising up to the smoke detector. Mr. Bulwark face palmed, then grabbed some baking soda and started throwing it on the flames. They went out almost immediately. Too late, as the fire alarm starting blaring throughout the school while everyone in class started cheering.

"Okay, everybody, single file out to the field! Last person close the door behind you!" Mr. Bulwark commanded. He looked at me, sighed, and shook his head. "Well, you got your wish, Chris. Cajun blackened crepes today!"

The whole school filed out to the field. I saw Rover across the way. I couldn't hear what he was saying, but he was frantically gesturing to people's belly buttons. I think he was trying to collect more lint. *Seriously, dude? I thought. Even during a fire??* I shook my head, and glanced over to the opposite side of the field.

Standing there on the grass, with a clipboard, was a

thin, grimy man, with a scraggly, coarse goatee. His suit hung off his frame almost like dirty rags, and it was an odd yellow color. He didn't seem to be in charge of any classroom, and as soon as the firefighters showed up, he went over to talk to them. He must be the principal. He reminded me of someone, but whom?

Suddenly, my mind flashed back to the horrible night my dad was brutally murdered. Once again, I saw the lab, I smelled the a rid smoke. It was HIM! The RAT STALKER! In my SCHOOL!

My mind clouded with rage! I felt almost like Bruce Banner turning into the Hulk. My face started twitching, and I could feel every eye muscle. I grinded my teeth together, tasting the metallic tang of blood as I bit my tongue. Muscles tightening, I felt like I needed to smash someone into the earth! I started to move towards the Rat Stalker with a vengeance, when all of a sudden, I felt a hand on my shoulder.

"Easy, Ninja Kid," Mr. Bulwark whispered, so quietly that no one else could hear. "Now is not the time." I looked at him in awe, suddenly deflated. He had a calming presence. "You are safe for now. Be calm and mindful."

"How? Why...?"

"I'll explain it all later," he said. The bell rang, and we were excused. "Later," said Mr. Bulwark, as he pushed me towards my next class.

CHAPTER 7

All day at school, I kept thinking, thinking, and thinking about the Rat Stalker. *What was he doing at my school? How did he find me? Who was Mr. Bulwark, and how did he know I was a Ninja Kid?* All these questions ran through my head and I couldn't concentrate on school at all. I think I failed a math test. I'm not even sure.

When I got home, I asked Mom, "Mom, what do you know about Mr. Bulwark?"

"Isn't he your fun Home Ec. teacher?"

"Yeah, but how does he know I'm Ninja Kid?"

"Stop being ridiculous! You're not a ninja. You're just a kid. Now, for the millionth time... go put your laundry away!"

"Mom! I'm a ninja! I'll prove it! Did you see me do that?" I asked.

"Do what?" said Mom.

"Exactly!" I said. That joke never gets old. Mom laughed.

"Laundry! Now!" she said, chuckling as she turned back to her computer to work.

I bent over to pick up my laundry basket, as frustrated as ever, and the lighter from my dad fell out of my pocket. As I went to get it, a rat jumped out of my laundry basket! It grabbed the lighter in its large yellow teeth and dragged it out the slightly open garage door. "Hey! Come back here, you little jerk!" I yelled at the rat. I chased after it, feeling like Rover chasing the rat in the park. I tried to squeeze through the opening in the garage door, but it was only 5 inches tall. I shouldn't have tried. I hurt my shoulder doing it. Hey... I never said I was a GOOD ninja. I pushed the button to raise

the garage all the way, wasting precious seconds while the rat ran further from my house.

The garage finally opened just far enough that I could crouch through. It was only seconds but it felt like minutes. I had to get that lighter back!

I saw the rat turning the corner on the other side of the sidewalk across the street. I sprinted after him, tripping over my floppy shoelaces and nearly falling as I ran. The sidewalk seemed even longer than usual. I got to the corner, and saw the rat running towards an idling black van with the door open. I could just make out the faded, scratched out letters E-X-T-E-R-M-I-N-A-T-O-R on the door. As I watched in horror, the rat jumped into the van while I saw an arm in a yellow sleeve slam the door shut behind it. The van took off with a shriek of the tires.

I then did something stupid. I grabbed the back of the van and jumped onto the bumper. All my ninja training had prepared me for almost anything, but riding on the top of a moving vehicle was something else! This was a whole other level of ninja! The wind started whipping through my hair, which obviously needed to be cut, as it was blowing right into my eyes. I could barely see as I started to crawl around the side of the van. The smell of diesel fuel filled my nose and caused me to choke and cough.

The van was turning and picking up speed, and it was hard to hold on. My fingers felt like they were slipping. As I was almost to the passenger door, the driver took an extremely sharp turn, no doubt an effort to try to throw me off. My feet flew off of the van, but my hands still had a slight grip. I went flying around the corner attached to the van like a rag doll. As the van straightened out, I thudded back against the door and hit my shin on the metal.

I looked in the window. There, I almost had a heart attack. My principal, the Rat Stalker, was driving the van and holding the lighter. *What does he want with my lighter?* I thought. I pulled open the door, and jumped in without thinking. I snatched the lighter from his greasy cracked hands and quickly jumped out of the moving van, rolling as I did. I had bad luck, and rolled right into a telephone pole. BANG! I bonked my head pretty good. But I didn't have time to pay attention to that. I got up, lighter in hand, and ran home as quickly as I could. The van drove off, screeching around the corner as it went.

CHAPTER 8

"Mom! You won't believe what just happened!" I gasped as I ran in the front door. "My lighter got stolen by a rat but I chased it and jumped on the back of a van and the principal was driving and he's the Rat Stalker who killed Dad and..." The words tumbled out of my mouth.

"Whoa! Hold on! Slow down, mister," Mom took my shoulders in her hands. "What's this bump on your head?"

"That's from where I jumped out of the van and hit my head on the pole! But I got my lighter back, see?" I held up the lighter to her face proudly.

"That bump looks pretty bad, and you're talking nonsense. I'm taking you to the doctor."

"Mom, no! I'm telling the truth!" But Mom wouldn't hear of it. She steered me to the car and dragged me off to get my head checked.

We got home late that night. My head was okay. Just a small bump, not a concussion. Mom still wouldn't believe my story though. She said if I was a ninja, I was the worst one ever. I went to bed as confused and frustrated as ever.

The next few weeks at home and school went by uneventfully, unless you count me getting in trouble for talking too much and being obnoxious in class. No ninjas, no rats. I didn't even see the Rat Stalker at school. I DID learn how to make snickerdoodles in Home Ec., so I guess that's pretty awesome. Mr. Bulwark avoided talking to me when other kids weren't around, and I eventually gave up trying to get him to tell me what he knew. I guess he changed his mind about wanting to talk to me. Rover and I tried to figure out why and how the Rat Stalker was back, to no avail. It seemed as if life was settling back to normal.

One day weeks later, after school, we were hanging out at the park again, and Rover pulled out his nasty jar of belly button lint. "Dude! Just throw that away! It's disgusting." I said.

"No, it's not! It's magical!" He declared. "As magical as a unicorn!" He began to prance around the playground saying belly button lint was the best thing that ever happened to him. There were a bunch of 8th graders hanging out nearby, and they began to notice Rover's weird behavior.

"Rover!" I hissed. "Stop that! Bad! People are watching! You're making us look weird!" Rover didn't stop.

In fact, he started dancing bigger and making up a song about his jar.

"It's the best thing that happened to me! It's a jar of belly button lint! Annnnnnd... I love it!" he sang, in a loud throaty voice.

"Rover! Cut that out!" I yelled at the top of my lungs. "You're WEIRD!" I yelled angrily. The whole playground turned and looked at us. Rover stopped, and his face dropped. He looked seriously offended.

"Fine then. If you don't accept me, I'll leave," Rover said quietly. He started walking across the grass towards his home.

"Rover, come back! You're just weird. It's cool! But you just can't be like that in public," I said.

"No. You're always making fun of me. No more. Bye, Chris," he said. Oh no. *Bye?* I thought. Rover had never, EVER, in his life just said bye whenhe left. It was always, "See you later, alligator," or "I'll be back" in a Terminator voice, or "Banzai!" He was really upset. I screwed up big time. I should've just watched in amusement, like everyone else. I should have accepted him for who he is. After all, weird is interesting! Much better than "normal." I watched in amazement as Rover slowly let the belly button lint jar drop from his hands, onto the grass.

I ran to pick it up. "Rover! Wait! I'm sorry!" But Rover just kept walking slowly away. I held the jar in utter disappointment. Rover was so upset. My stomach felt like it was sinking. I had to make this right. I started to follow him.

Rover reached the edge of the park, and was turning towards home, when a black van sharply curved the corner. THAT black van... the one the Rat Stalker was driving when the rat stole my lighter! The van slowed as it neared Rover, the side door opened with a loud creak, and a hand reached out of the van and grabbed Rover. With supernatural strength, the Rat Stalker pulled him inside! The door slammed shut with a loud bang. With a squeal of the tires, the van drove away, taking Rover with it. The park was suddenly still and quiet.

I stood there in shock, speechless. My mind couldn't even process what I had just seen. What to do? What to do? I ran home as fast as I could to tell my mom what had happened.

CHAPTER 9

I made it home in record time. Like 3 minutes. As I got to the front door, I yanked it open like my life depended on it, and ran inside. In the living room, I found my mom. She was crying. Big messy tears were dripping out of her hazel eyes, which looked just like mine. Bok Choy was licking them off her. She was startled when she saw me. "What are you doing here?? How did you get here?" Her tears dried as she yelled at me. "I didn't pick you up from the park! That's not safe!"

"Actually, it's perfectly safe! I'm a ninja! But that's beside the point! Rover was kidnapped! And, why are you crying?" The words tumbled out of me. "And... we have to help Rover! Is it because of Dad? It's because of Dad, isn't it? That's why you're crying. I miss him, too! We have to get Rover back!" The words just kept coming, spilling out in a nonsensical way.

"Chris! STOP!" Mom said sternly as she put her hands on her hips. Her eyes narrowed, and her lips pursed, like my 5th grade teacher's used to. I was instantly silenced,

as all words left my mind. Her glare was frightening me. "Christopher. You are NOT allowed to go back and forth to the park alone."

"But Mom! It's Rover! He's in trouble...!"

"And so are you. And DON'T call me Butt Mom." She looked totally serious this time, instead of joking like she usually did. "Because you disobeyed me, you are grounded for a week. And no electronics. Or phone. The only time you can leave is for school, to which I'LL drive you."

"Are you kidding me?! Rover is in danger! "

"I don't care! Go to your room! No more of your stories! And stop with your ninjas and vans and all that!"

I started to protest once more. I was silenced as Mom pointed her fingers towards the stairs. "To your room!"

I didn't bother to fight. She wasn't backing down. I was still looking back at her angrily as I once again tripped over laundry sitting at the base of the stairs. I knew Mom was serious when she didn't even crack a smile.

As I sat in my room, staring at my ninja poster on the wall, Bok Choy comforting me with her head on my knee, my first thought was, *That poster is rad.* My second thought was, *How could I let this happen?? How will I rescue Rover? Where is he? Is he okay?* I sat for a long time, hoping Rover was still okay, was still alive. My eyes grew grainy and tired. I finally fell asleep staring at a leaping ninja about halfway up the wall after who knows how long.

I awoke from a dead sleep, groggy, the sun glaring through my window like it does right before it sets for the night. I could see dust motes dancing in the rays. A sharp, startling noise made me realize what had awakened me from my impromptu nap.

The phone. It was ringing. And Mom wasn't picking it up. Where was she? "Mom? The phone...?" No answer. I walked out to the hall. "Mom?" Nothing. I shrugged my shoulders. I wasn't supposed to use the phone, but Mom wasn't answering. I picked it up. "Hello?"

CHAPTER 10

"Hello, Ninja Kid," said a distinctly scratchy voice. I could hardly believe who had called. It was the Rat Stalker! "We have your friend."

"Where is he?" I shouted into the phone. "Give me back my best friend! Give me back Rover!" I was so angry I kicked the old stairway banister. I forgot my ninja training, and I kicked so hard it broke and fell down the stairs. Oops. Mom was going to be mad about that one.

Rat Stalker made a weird screeching sound into the phone. "You want your friend back? Meet me at school tomorrow, before it starts. And bring your dad's lighter!"

"The lighter? What? Why the lighter?" I asked.

"Just bring it! Bring it and I'll give you back your canine!" He said with a sneer in his voice. "And don't tell ANYONE! Or you can say goodbye to your little pet!" He laughed wickedly as the phone went dead.

Just then, I heard the front door open. I put the phone down and ran back into my room, so Mom wouldn't see me out. I was supposed to be grounded in my room!

Unfortunately, I forgot about the broken banister.

"Chris!" She had spotted it. Oh no! As if I wasn't in enough trouble already. Maybe I could blame this one on Bok Choy. She hadn't taken one for the team in a while. I jumped back into bed and pretended to be asleep. I could hear rapid footsteps running up the stairs. It sounded like more than just my mom. "Chris! Are you okay?" She rushed into my room. I pretended to wake up.

"Oh, what?" I said groggily. She seemed flustered and appeared to buy my act. Behind her, unexpectedly, was Mr. Bulwark! "Mr. Bulwark!" I exclaimed. "Why the heck are you here?"

"First things first," he said. "Are you okay? We saw the broken banister! Did you get attacked?"

"By what? What are you talking about, broken banister? It must've been the dog." I started to call Bok Choy into the room.

"Don't worry about that." Mom said. "I'm just glad you're okay. I ran into Mr. Bulwark here when I went to the market while you were asleep. We got to talking about your stories. Turns out, you weren't lying." Mom and Mr. Bulwark then explained to me how he had known my dad all those years ago in Japan. Mr. Bulwark had worked with Dad, and had been there the night of the fire. He had seen it all. Mr. Bulwark knew one day, the Rat Stalker would come for us, and come for Dad's information. He had gotten the job at my middle school to keep an eye on me when he found out the Rat Stalker became the principal there. The only question was... where was Dad's information hidden?

All that explained a lot. No wonder Mr. Bulwark knew I was a ninja! I thought about telling Mom and Mr. Bulwark about Rover, but I decided to keep my mouth shut. I couldn't risk anything happening to him. I would have to fight this battle on my own.

Mr. Bulwark ended up staying for dinner. Then he stayed late. Then he stayed later. It got so late, I went up to my room to get ready for bed. He and Mom were so engaged in conversation they didn't even notice when

I left the room. I could hear them downstairs, talking and laughing. They seemed to be really happy together. I decided to tune them out and figure out what to do in the morning.

Okay... I'll get there 40 minutes before school. I'll tell Mom I have to work on an extra credit project so she brings me early. Once I see the Rat Stalker, who will probably have ninjas with him, I'll charge him and catch him out of nowhere, roundhouse, and kick him in the face! Then I'll take on the ninjas, and rescue Rover. Then Rover and I will jump up and down on the Rat Stalker's unconscious body! I'll even let him celebrate with his jar of belly button lint, so he knows I think being weird is okay.

These were my immediate thoughts. Unfortunately, as I was to find out in about 8 hours, things didn't go that way at all.

CHAPTER 11

HIYA! My ninja alarm clock woke me with its battle cry a little before dawn. It was time to get ready. I dug through the back of my closet, and found my old Halloween costume. My ninja costume. Might as well look the part! I put it on, looked in the mirror, and realized the last time I had worn this costume, I had been eight and in the third grade. It was way too small! My arms and legs jutted out from all openings, and a sliver of my stomach was showing. *Verrrry threatening*, I thought sarcastically. I laughed to myself as I took off the ninja outfit, and put on a pair of cargo shorts and a baseball t-shirt. Okay, not so scary, but at least I could move!

I then grabbed the jar of belly button lint, and crammed it into my pocket. In other pockets went ninja stars, and a pack of bubble gum, for a victory chew with Rover when this mess was done. Last but not least, I tucked Dad's lighter into my back pocket. I wasn't planning to show it to Rat Stalker, because I planned to knock him unconscious. I tucked it in there simply

because I always carried it for good luck.

I ran downstairs to tell Mom it was time to go.

CHAPTER 12

We pulled up to the school early in the morning, and Mom let me out of the car. There was no one around. The school was deserted. But I knew the Rat Stalker had to be hiding here somewhere, with Rover. I watched Mom drive off, and then got to work.

I went around the back of the school, so no one could see me from the street. I scaled the chain link fence quickly. My shoelace caught on a loose link on the other side, and I fell to the grass on my face. *Some ninja I am,* I thought. I got up, brushed myself off, and rushed over to the nearest hallway to have a look around.

The first hallway was filled with 6th grade lockers. I started to move stealthily through the corridor. Halfway down, I noticed one locker hanging slightly open. It was mine. It had been pried open, and all my stuff was gone. At the back, there was one sticky note stuck on the locker wall. I read:

Your school materials are in my office. Come here immediately. Signed, The Principal

I carefully walked to his office. I knew it had to be a trap, so instead of sneaking in, as he would expect from a Ninja Kid, I decided to run right in the front door. I held my fist in front of me, and burst through the office door! "Banzai!" Oh crap! I ran right smack into something super sticky and as big as me! Darn it! My head, body, and arms and legs were all stuck tightly to the substance and I couldn't move! My face felt like it was super glued in place. It was a giant rat glue trap! I heard footsteps walking towards me, although I couldn't turn to see who it was. But I had a pretty good idea.

"Hello, Ninja Kid," I heard the Rat Stalker say in his squeaky voice. "Nice of you to pay me a visit. I thought you might try to outsmart me. But guess what? I out-smarted you! Like a rat in a trap, but a lot easier! You see, I'm always one step ahead of you!"

I struggled to get free. "WHmmmmm Rhrrrr? Whhrt hvv uuuu dnn oo mm?" It came out a just a little muffled, as my lips were stuck tight to the trap. Rat Stalker rolled his eyes, grabbed the back of my head, and yanked my head off the rat trap with a ripping sound. "OW!" I exclaimed. "What the heck, dude?"

"You were saying?" the Rat Stalker asked.

"Where's Rover? What have you done to him?" *Better,* I thought.

"That's for me to know, and you to find out! Now, where's the lighter?" The Rat Stalker asked eagerly.

This was not going how I had planned at all. I was stuck tight in the Rat Stalker/principal's office, I didn't know where Rover was, and this guy was going to take my dad's lighter! Where were my ninja skills now?

Suddenly, the door behind me opened with a crash! Mr. Bulwark and Mom rushed in. "Get away from my boy, you rat!" Mom exclaimed. As Mom tore me off the glue trap, Mr. Bulwark went all ninja on the Rat Stalker. He started to kick him in the face and knock him around the room. Mom and I stopped for a second, and just watched in amazement. Mr. Bulwark was a butt kicker! He really WAS a cool guy!

Just as it looked like the Rat Stalker was about to go down, a weird noise from the next room distracted all of us. It sounded like a dog yelping in pain, but also like a car crash. Mom, Mr. Bulwark, and I looked over to see what it was. As we did, the Rat Stalker grabbed my lighter from my pocket and ran out the door. In the next room, we glimpsed Rover tied to a chair that had crashed down on the floor. He had tried to free himself and had fallen. That's what the noise was!

"You guys rescue Rover! I'll handle the Rat Stalker!" I yelled, as I ran out of the room after him.

"Go for it, Ninja Kid!" my mom said. I smiled and turned around.

"Thanks, Mom!" I gave her a wink, and took off after the Rat Stalker. "Banzai!"

He was running down the hallway towards the cafeteria. The school gates had just opened, and there were kids starting to show up to school in the hallways. The Stalker was dodging them. Kids who knew him as the principal were saying hi to him, but he was ignoring them, clutching the lighter. He put it in his pocket as he ran.

The Rat Stalker ran into the cafeteria, and I raced in after him. I could see the lunch ladies busy preparing much of the food for the day. The Rat Stalker was already at the back door, which led to the parking lot. He was trying to open it, but it was locked. He kept trying, but no go. He had left his keys in the office. Yes!

"This is it, Rat Stalker. Game over. Give me the lighter, and you won't get hurt. You don't, and I hurt you!" I threatened.

"Like you can beat me, kid. Ha!" He charged at me, arms swinging. I dodged him easily, and I elbow striked him. Well, that was my plan, anyways. I actually hit the fire alarm on the wall instead, setting it off. Loud, piercing alarms started ringing throughout the school. We both looked up in surprise at the noise. "Nice going," he said sarcastically. "Second time you've set that alarm off this year. Your ninja training has served you well!" He made a little bow to me. As he did, I noticed the lighter fall quietly out of his pocket onto the floor. The Rat Stalker didn't notice.

Kids started running into the lunchroom in response to the alarm, heading for the back door. As they swarmed us, the Rat Stalker turned and headed towards the front door to get away. I couldn't get to him through the surge of kids. I had to stop him! I could only think of one thing. Something I had always wanted to do. At the top of my lungs, I put my hands to my mouth, and yelled

"FOOD FIGHT!!!"

All the kids stopped running, grabbed a plate from the line, and the food started flying! I saw spaghetti hit a girl right in the face, and she slurped it right up, and then gagged! A plate of macaroni and something that could've been cheese, except for the fact that it was blue, zoomed over my head and hit a window behind me. The Tuesday Surprise thrown by an 8th grade girl hit the wall, burned a hole in it, and kept going. The Rat Stalker was slowed down in the chaos, but he was still too far away for me to catch. I threw an extremely brown banana at him, and hit him in the back. It didn't even faze him. All it did was get his shirt dirty. I had to stop him, but how?

Suddenly, I thought of the lighter. I reached down and picked it up, and it was glowing. I heard a voice behind me. "Whoa! That can't be normal." I turned around,

and there was Rover!

"Rover! You're safe! Awesome! We good?" Rover nodded. "No time to talk. We have to stop the Rat Stalker!" I yelled over the din of the food fight. "He's way over there!" Rover noticed the jar of belly button lint shoved in my pocket, and reached to pull it out.

"I have an idea," he said, looking at the jar. He unscrewed the lid, tossed it to the floor, and held the jar towards me.

"Wha...? Not NOW, Rover! Put your belly button lint away!" I couldn't believe he was at it again.

"No! The lighter! Light the lint on fire. It's the only way!" My face lit up in realization of his plan. It was brilliant! It was a stink bomb! I held the lighter to the jar in his out stretched hands, and the jar lit up immediately and started to smoke furiously. "Ahhhhhhh!" we screamed. "Get rid of it! Get rid of it!" It smelled... well, I can't even describe it. It was so nasty, it made the Tuesday Surprise smell like sweet, springtime flowers.

We threw the jar across the cafeteria, just in front of the Rat Stalker. It landed with a crash, and smoke billowed all around him. He started to cough and choke and spasm, and then he fell to the floor with a thud. We thought he might be dead.

CHAPTER 13

After the smoke cleared in the room, the police arrived, and they arrested the Rat Stalker. He wasn't dead after all; he had just fainted from the smell. As they dragged him off to jail, Rover and I turned to Mom and Mr. Bulwark, who were now holding hands, and asked, "How did you know this would happen?"

"We had a feeling after you were acting so strangely last night. We decided to follow you."

"Why did the Rat Stalker want the lighter so badly?" I asked.

Mr. Bulwark put his hand out. "I figured it out when I saw the lighter. Let me show you." As Mom and I watched in amazement, Mr. Bulwark popped off the back end, and something small slipped out into his hand. "He was looking for this." He handed me a flash drive. "On there is your Dad's entire work. This contains the information on how to alter the rat genes so that they may help the world."

"His research wasn't lost after all!" Mom exclaimed.

"Wow! My dad was pretty radical! He thought of everything!" Mom, Rover, and Mr. Bulwark smiled in agreement.

The vice principal of the school then walked over. "Thank you, Ninja Kid, for saving us from the Rat Stalker! I never trusted him. Now, while we clean up this mess and the police collect evidence, school is cancelled for the rest of the day." All the kids cheered.

I looked at Rover. "Well, what do you want to do, instead?"

Rover looked at me, and then looked at my mom. "Do you think you could drive us to the park?"

Mom smiled at us, glanced at Mr. Bulwark, and said, "You know what, boys? I have a better idea. Go ahead and ride your bikes there! You're a Ninja Kid, Chris. I think it'll be okay."

Rover and I looked at each other in surprise, big grins breaking out on our faces. This was turning out to be a pretty great school year. We high fived.

"BANZAI!"

About the authors:

Deb Patterson and Cole Patterson are a mother/son team who got the idea for The Adventures of Ninja Kid one spring morning in 2015 during an inspired and animated talk about defeating ninjas in the kitchen with a chewed up bagel! With much laughter and little planning, they spent that summer while Cole was between 5th and 6th grades creating the book. Deb spends her time as an interior designer and full time mom, while Cole's interests range from soccer to acting to video games... and, of course, snickerdoodle cookies! They live in Southern California with Deb's hubby aka Cole's dad, a big brother, and 2 crazy dogs, with plans to move to Colorado soon.

About the illustrator:

Katie Heady is an art student from Columbia, Maryland. Katie loves owls, deer, corgis, and cats. Katie is majoring in Computer Animation at Ringling College of Art and Design. She hopes to gain super powers in the future.

Made in the USA
San Bernardino, CA
27 September 2016